Jungle Jam Chapter Books

The Bear Who Wouldn't Share

Jungle Jam Chapter Books: The Bear Who Wouldn't Share
© MMII by Fancy Monkey Studios, Inc.

Visit us at FancyMonkey.com.

"The Bear Who Wouldn't Share" and "A Monkey's Uncle"
written by Nathan Carlson
illustrations by Matthew Bates
cover design by Messy Studio, Los Angeles

ISBN 1-59269-001-7

Manufactured in the United States of America

The Bear Who Wouldn't Share

Romans 12:13

Chapter One

The Bible says in Romans 12:13 that we should share with those in need and practice hospitality. That's a lesson Gruffy Bear needed to learn on the day of our story.

It all started when Millard the monkey joined Gruffy on a camping trip. "Make sure you bring enough food for at least five days," said Gruffy. He loved camping.

"Don't worry," said Millard. "I wasn't

4.

born yesterday."

The next morning, Millard packed his sleeping bag, his pillow, a flashlight, a swimsuit, a snorkel and a roll of duck tape. "In case I see any broken ducks," he said.

He started to leave. "Oops. I almost forgot." Millard grabbed a banana and headed out the door. All that packing had made him hungry. So he ate his banana on the way to Gruffy's.

Gruffy was waiting when Millard arrived. "Got everything?" Gruffy said.

"Yes, sir. I made a list."

"Atta monkey." The two campers headed out.

After walking a few hours, they were hungry. "This is a good time to stop for lunch," said Gruffy.

"I've been starving since we left," said Millard.

Gruffy carefully unpacked his lavish picnic. Millard sat and watched. "Why aren't you getting out your lunch, Millard? You did remember to bring food didn't you?"

"Of course I did."

Gruffy lifted a large and delicious-looking sandwich to his mouth.

"Except," said Millard, "I already ate it."

"What?!" said Gruffy.

"On my way to your cave."

"You ate five days worth of food?"

"It was slightly less than five days worth,"

said Millard. "It was a banana."

Gruffy growled. "We'll miss lunchtime completely if we walk back now." He growled again. "All right, I'll share my lunch with you."

"Thanks," said Millard. He grabbed the sandwich out of Gruffy's hand. Gruffy was shocked at how fast Millard gobbled it up. Before Gruffy could stop him, Millard ate the entire lunch.

"That's it!" said Gruffy. "This camping trip is over!"

"But you've got four-and-a-half days worth of food left," said Millard. "Say, are those potato chips in that bag?"

"Keep your greedy hands to yourself."

"Don't worry. I'm almost full."

"Almost?" said Gruffy. "What's wrong with you, Millard?"

"Nothing that a bag of chips can't fix. And maybe those thin mint cookies."

Gruffy wasn't about to spend the rest of his trip watching Millard eat. Especially since the only food left was Gruffy's. He gathered his things and turned to head back.

Millard quickly slipped the chips out of Gruffy's backpack and followed behind. The camping trip was over.

Gruffy decided he would never take Millard camping again. The next week Millard even promised to bring enough food for both of them. But Gruffy still said no.

He would do his camping alone.

Millard sadly headed back to his tree house. On the way, he saw Nozzles the elephant. "Hey, Millard. Glad I ran into you. I hope you and Gruffy aren't going camping today. The radio said a bad storm is coming."

"Don't worry," said Millard. "I'm not."

"Good. It's far too dangerous." Nozzles walked off.

"Glad I'm not going," said Millard. "Wait a minute. I'm not going but Gruffy is. He shouldn't be out in that storm alone. I'd better

8.

go with him."

But Gruffy didn't believe Millard. "What? There's not a single cloud in the sky. This couldn't be a more perfect camping day."

"I'm worried about you, Gruffy," said Millard. "I won't let you go out in that storm alone! Say, are those berry tarts in that bag?"

"Thanks," said Gruffy. "I'm sure I'll be fine. I might get a little wet, but at least the storm won't eat all my food." He turned and headed off.

"Gruffy, wait!" said Millard. "You could get hurt! Say, were those cheese crackers I saw in that box?!"

Chapter Two

Gruffy happily walked along snacking on the cheese crackers. In fact, they tasted better than ever. Soon he was enjoying lovely views he'd never seen before.

Suddenly huge, dark clouds began to fill the sky. "Whoa," said Gruffy. "I'd better camp here for the night." He quickly set up his tent and climbed inside. And not a moment too soon. The rain began to pour down.

"Hi, there, Mr. Friendly bear," said a voice.

Gruffy was startled. He turned and noticed two little ants huddling in the corner.

"Looks like quite a storm," one said.

"Hey, what are you two doing in my tent?" said Gruffy.

"I'm Lenny," the ant said.

"I'm Filmore," said the other.

"We're sharing ants," they said together.

"Sharing ants?" said Gruffy.

"That's right," said Lenny. "If we had anything to share, we'd happily share it with you."

Filmore nodded. "It's just who we are."

"We're heading to a big party with our sharing-ant friends," said Lenny. "It's tomorrow. They'll have lots of stuff to share."

"You should come," Filmore said.

Just then, *kablam!* The thunder startled both the ants and Gruffy. The ants began to shiver.

"Wow, it's really getting bad out there," said Lenny.

"And cold," said Filmore.

"Yeah," said Gruffy. "I hate to say this but I guess you should be going now."

Ka-boom! went another blast of thunder. This one was even longer and louder then the first.

"D-do w-we really have to g-go?" said Lenny.

"O-out there?" said Filmore.

"Sorry, guys," said Gruffy. "It's a one-bear tent. My hands are tied."

"Can't we just stay until the storm passes?" said Filmore.

Gruffy pointed to a tag on the tent flap. It read, "One-Bear Tent."

"Good thing there's only one bear in here," said Filmore. "We promise not to take up much room."

"We could just crouch down in the corner," said Lenny.

"No way," said Gruffy. "'One-Bear tent' means no ants. If I share my tent, before long

12.

I'm sharing my food. It starts with ants. But mark my words. It ends with a monkey and a hungry bear."

"Say, are those sugar cookies in that box?" asked Lenny.

"Forget it," said Gruffy. "This is mine."

A flash of lightning lit up the tent. The rain came down so hard it sounded like rocks smacking the top of the tent.

The ants looked up at Gruffy. Tears filled their little eyes. "Please let us stay," they begged. "Please, Mr. Kind Bear?"

"The name's Gruffy Bear. You two take care now." Gruffy took a nice big bite out of a sugar cookie and pushed the ants out with his big toe. Then he quickly closed the tent flap and zipped it tight. "Cute little guys," he said, finishing the cookie. He rolled out his sleeping bag and drifted off to sleep.

The storm outside grew stronger by the minute. The wind blew in violent gusts. The rain came down even harder. Huge puddles formed on the ground.

A giant gust of wind blasted Gruffy's tent. It ripped apart and the pieces flew high into the night sky. Gruffy's camping gear was flung in every direction!

Another big blast of thunder! More wind and rain! Yet, one noise rose above it all.

"Zzzzzzz."

14.

Chapter Three

The bright afternoon sun beat down on Gruffy's face waking him.

"Wow. That was the best sleep I've had in a long time." Gruffy looked up toward the sun. "I can't believe I slept in. I've got to get going!"

He reached for his map. It wasn't there. Then he noticed something. "Everything's gone! My backpack, my flashlight, my first aid kit, my tent and even my duck tape in case I see any broken ducks."

Gruffy panicked. "My food! Where's my food?! I wasn't even hungry until I noticed it was missing. Now I'm starving."

He looked around again. "Whoa! I'm also lost. Some camping trip this is turning out to be." Gruffy glanced down. He noticed what looked like a piece of paper under a rock. "My map! I'm saved!" He quickly picked it up and read it.

"'One-Bear Tent.'"

He tossed the paper on the ground and started walking. He walked and walked for several hours. Then he stopped.

"I've got to go back and pick up my litter. Oh boy. Now where is it?" Gruffy walked for a few more hours. "It's no use. I'm so hungry I can't even think straight. Unless I think about food. Then I'm clear as a bell."

Gruffy was determined to press on. With all his might he tried to stay focused. "'One-Bear tent.' 'One-Bear tent.'"

Suddenly, Gruffy stopped. He saw

something in the distance. He started to walk again, this time a little faster. The closer he got, the more it looked like some kind of party. And that meant only one thing.

"Food! Every party has food."

Gruffy started running toward the party. He tried as hard as he could. But he was so tired, he could only take small steps.

His legs felt like they would give out at any moment. "Must... keep... going. Party... food... drink... hats..."

Finally his knees buckled. He fell to the ground with a thud.

18.

Chapter Four

After a few minutes, Gruffy managed to raise his head. He was closer to the party than he thought. He could see the guests in the distance. They were having a great time playing games, singing, eating and wearing hats.

Then Gruffy noticed something strange. This was no ordinary party. And it wasn't nearly as far away as it looked.

This was an ant party. And it was right under his nose!

There were lots of colorful balloons and streamers. Thousands of ants gathered around long tables. They filled their plates with food.

The next sound Gruffy heard was like music to his ears.

"Would you like something to eat?" said a friendly ant. "There's plenty here,"

"Oh, thank you," said Gruffy. "I'm so hungry."

"I'll fix a plate for you," said the ant. "Hat?"

"Sure," said Gruffy. "Thanks. This is quite a party. What are you celebrating?"

"Well, it started out as our annual sharing-ant party."

"We're sharing ants," said another ant.

"It's just who we are," said the first ant.

"But then," said the other ant, "something wonderful happened. Actually, something terrible and then something wonderful."

"Two of our friends got caught in the storm," said the first ant. "A mean, selfish monster wouldn't even let them stay in his tent."

"That's when the wonderful thing happened," said one of the ants. "Lenny and Filmore were rescued by the kindest, bravest, most generous soul."

"He saved their lives," said the other ant. "He gave them some of his food and brought them here. He's our hero."

"So now this party is for him, too," said another ant.

"Wow," said Gruffy, trying to get the little hat strap around his chin. "I'd like to meet this hero. Where is he?"

"Looking for his friend. The hero was very worried. He said he might come back for our help if he needed us."

The first ant handed Gruffy a plate full of sandwiches.

"Thank you." Gruffy raised the tiny sandwiches to his mouth. But before he could take his first bite -

"That's him!" shouted an ant from the crowd.

It was Lenny. He pointed at Gruffy. "He's the monster who kicked us out of his tent!"

"Ahhh!" screamed the ants.

Chapter Five

"Stop him! He's eating our food!" said Lenny.

"Freeze, Monster!" said Filmore. He scribbled something quickly on a piece of paper. Gruffy read the tiny printing.

"This is a 90,000-ant party!"

"That means no bears!" said Lenny. "Sorry. Our hands are tied."

"He's the one we told you about," Filmore shouted to the other ants. "He wouldn't share his food with us. Now you're sharing our food with him!"

"Wait." Gruffy gobbled up the tiny sandwiches. Then with his mouth still full, he said, "I can explain."

Lenny quickly grabbed Gruffy's plate. It was too late for the sandwiches but at least the little ant had saved some chips. The crowd became an angry mob. They started yelling and throwing tiny crescent rolls at him.

"Stop it!" said Gruffy. "That tickles!"

Then a voice called out over the noisy crowd, "Stop! Stop!" The angry ants did.

"Look at us. What are we doing?!" said a tiny ant. "This isn't who we are. We're sharing-ants, not angry-selfish-fighting-ants."

"The bear didn't share with us," said Lenny.

"Yes," said the tiny ant. "But we share because it's right to be kind and generous."

"That's true," said another ant.

"It's just who we are," said a third.

"Remember, we don't share because we're sharing-ants. We're sharing-ants because we share," said the tiny ant. "We shouldn't change who we are because of who he is! Besides, we're wasting perfectly good crescent rolls. Now let's get a hold of ourselves."

Just then, a voice from behind Gruffy said, "Here you are. I've been looking all over for you."

"Our hero!" shouted the ants.

Gruffy turned around. "Millard? This is your hero?"

"That's him," said one of the ants.

"Wait," said Millard. "This is the monster?"

"That's him," said another ant.

"Millard, what are you doing out here?" said Gruffy.

"Looking for you. I was worried."

"Worried about my cheese crackers, you mean," said Gruffy.

"No. I was worried about you, Gruffy. In

fact, I brought plenty of food for both of us."
Millard opened his pack. Every inch was packed
with yummy food.

A little ant licked his lips and looked at
Millard. "We're sharing ants."

"It's just who they are," said Gruffy. "I'm
sorry, Millard. I should have given you a second
chance. You really are a good friend. And
Lenny, Filmore, I was wrong not to share with
you. I hope you can forgive me."

"Sure," said Filmore. Lenny handed
Gruffy back his plate of chips.

"We forgive you, Monster," said the ants.

"Me too, Monster," said Millard.

"Listen," said Gruffy. "All you guys are
welcome to visit me in the jungle anytime. You
can stay in my cave when it rains."

"Yeah, um, we do that anyway," said a tiny
ant.

"Shhh," said the others.

Millard and Gruffy stayed and enjoyed the
sharing-ant party for a while. Then they headed

back.

   "Look," said Millard.

   "A broken duck," said Gruffy.

   So they fixed it and went home.

A Monkey's Uncle

Malachi 1:14

Chapter One

God hates it when we cheat. In fact, the Bible says in Malachi 1:14 that a cheater is cursed. That's a lesson the Jungle Jam Gang learned the hard way.

It all started when a friendly-looking police monkey called up to Millard's tree house. "Looks like you got some mail, Millard!" he said and walked on.

Millard raced down to his mailbox and found an invitation inside. "Wow!" he said. "I hardly ever get invited to anything."

Just then Nozzles the elephant walked by.
"You'd better hurry, Millard. You'll be late for
the picnic."

"What picnic?"

"Oops. I thought Gruffy Bear invited
everybody. Never mind."

"Who cares?" said Millard. "I got
something better!" Millard handed the letter to
Nozzles.

"'Dear Monkey Monthly reader,'" said
Nozzles. "'Good news! It's that time of year
again. Time for our first annual Uncle/Nephew
Monkey Banquet. A centuries-old tradition.
This year there will be a door-prize drawing for
one of the uncles. Just like every year.'"

"Who's ever heard of a door prize at a
banquet?" said Millard.

"Your Uncle Nozzles," said Nozzles.

"Oh that's right. They do that every year.
But you're not a monkey."

"I'm not your uncle, either. But I do love
door prizes." Nozzles looked at the letter. "'If

your real uncle can't come -- '"

"And he never can," said Millard.

"'You can bring a stand-in. And he doesn't have to be a monkey. But the nephew must be. After all, it is a monkey banquet.'"

"After all," said Millard.

"'Remember, the banquet is just five days from now. Give or take three or four. Depending on when you receive this letter. Black tie and tail required. Pants optional.'"

"Great," said Millard.

Nozzles turned the envelope over. "Hey, this is addressed to Marvin J. Monkey."

"Yeah, that's me. I've also been Markie, Maynard, Morrie and Melissa. The first year, the magazine is free. After that you have to change your name to get it free."

"Isn't that cheating?" said Nozzles.

"Didn't you mention something about a door prize?" said Millard.

"I can go as 'Nozzles,' right?"

"Of course," said Millard. "This year."

"Okay, 'Marvin.' Whatever gets your Uncle Nozzles that door prize."

Just then Sully ran up. "Door prize! Count me in."

"Sorry, Sully. I can only bring one uncle."

"That's Uncle Sully to you, little buddy."

Gruffy and Racquet the skunk came running up the path. "Did someone say door prize?!"

"You're all too late," said Nozzles. "'Marvin' is taking me."

"What?" said Sully. "Did Nozzles offer you free piggy-back rides, 'Marvin'?"

"Did Sully offer you free elevator service?" said Nozzles.

"How about a bottomless pot of tea and all the crumpets you can eat?" said Racquet.

"That tree-house roof of yours still leaking? 'Cause your Uncle Gruffy will have it fixed in a jiffy," said Gruffy.

All the wonderful offers gave Millard an idea. "Starting tomorrow, you can each have one day to be my uncle. Then I'll choose my favorite."

That door prize is as good as mine, thought Gruffy, Nozzles, Racquet and Sully.

Let the games begin, thought Millard.

Chapter Two

The next morning, Millard woke to the bright sun shining in his face. He opened his eyes. The roof of his tree house was – gone!

"Found the leak," said Gruffy.

"Me too," said Millard, looking at the blue sky.

"There was a tiny crack in the corner. It could be patched. Well, could have been. But my nephew deserves a whole new roof. And a skylight and ceiling fan."

"Wow! Is that fresh berry pie I smell?"

"Yup," said Gruffy. "And that's just this hour's pie."

"Uncle Gruffy," said Millard, "I love you."

The next morning, Nozzles arrived. "Good morning, Millard. How's my favorite nephew?"

Millard stepped out of his tree house and looked down at Nozzles. "Good morning, Uncle Nozzles."

Nozzles lifted his elephant trunk up to Millard. "Welcome to Uncle Nozzles' Elevator

Service," said Nozzles. "Make yourself comfortable."

"Thank you," said Millard. He climbed onto Nozzles' trunk and sat down. "Very comfy."

"Going down."

"I thought we'd spend the day stocking up on coconuts," said Millard.

"Your wish is my command, little buddy."

"Then I wish we'd quit yakking and start stocking up on coconuts," said Millard. "You uncles are so chatty."

"First floor." Nozzles lowered Millard to the ground.

"I have to get off?"

"I guess not. The coconut tree is right here," said Nozzles. He turned and lifted Millard. "Going up."

"Whee!" said Millard.

"You know, if I flip my head back quickly," said Nozzles, "you could get the big coconuts at the top of the tree."

"Whee," said Millard, flying into the air.

"That's the kind of thing favorite uncles do!" said Nozzles.

"So is this," said Gruffy, holding up a fresh berry pie.

"Hey," said Nozzles. "Your turn was yesterday. You're cheating."

Millard crashed to the ground. "Ouch."

"I'm just bringing my nephew some pie," said Gruffy. "And a bandage. If that be cheating, then cheater I be." *That door prize is as good as mine,* thought Gruffy.

We'll see about that, thought Nozzles.

"Then cheater I be?" thought Millard.

Chapter Three

The next morning, Millard woke to loud banging on his door.

"Breakfast in bed for my favorite nephew," said Racquet, walking in.

44.

"Thanks, Uncle Racquet. I'm starved."

"You'll probably want to wash those crumpets down with some coconut milk," said Nozzles, walking in.

"Who wants pie?" said Gruffy, walking in.

"You guys are cheating," said Racquet. "This is Sully's day."

Just then Sully walked in. "Good morning, nephew – hey!"

"That's what I was just saying," said Racquet. "Hey!"

"You guys are all cheating!" said Sully.

"If this be cheating…" said Gruffy and Nozzles.

"Crumpet?" said Racquet.

"Don't mind if I do," said Sully.

"Coconut milk?" said Nozzles.

"Yes," said Sully. "And some pie. Just a sliver. I'm watching my weight."

"Hello?!" Millard waved his hands in the air. "It's awfully crowded in here."

"Yeah," said Racquet. "Who invited the

monkey? Oops. Crumpet, Millard?"

"Don't give me that 'crumpet' nonsense," said Millard. He sniffed the air. "On the other hand, give me that crumpet."

"Nonsense!" said Gruffy. "Have some pie."

"Don't mind if I do," said Racquet.

"You're going to want some coconut milk with that," said Nozzles.

"Thanks." Racquet took a sip. "Mmmm. Crumpet?"

"Sure," said Nozzles.

"Gruffy, this pie is great." Sully took a big bite.

"Hello?!" said Millard.

"Who let the monkey in?" said Gruffy. "Oops. Pie, Millard?"

"Don't give me that 'pie' nonsense," said Millard. He sniffed the air. "On the other hand, give me some pie."

"Nonsense," said Nozzles. "Have some coconut milk."

46.

"Don't mind if I do," said Gruffy.

"A crumpet would go nicely with that," said Racquet.

"Thanks," said Gruffy.

"Hey, pass the pie," said Nozzles.

"I love the cinnamon in the crumpets, Racquet," said Sully.

"Hello?!" said Millard.

"Are you still here, Millard?" said Sully. "Oops. Piggy-back ride?"

"Don't give me that 'piggy-back ride' nonsense," said Millard. "But do give me the crumpets, pie and coconut milk. And then get out of my house! All of you!"

"But it's my day to be uncle," said Sully.

"I know. Piggy-back rides," said Millard. "Got it. I'll let you know who my favorite uncle is tomorrow. Right now I just want some peace and quiet."

The animals turned to go.

Another crumpet? thought Racquet.

Don't mind if I do, thought Nozzles.

Chapter Four

The next morning the animals gathered at
the clearing. "Hi, guys," said Millard.

"Blah blah blah," said Sully. "Let's hear
your decision already."

"Let them down easy," said Gruffy. "They
all tried hard. At least most of them did. Well,
some. Me."

"You've been very good uncles," said
Millard. "Except for the fact that you all
cheated. And if there's one thing monkeys can't

stand it's cheating."

"But you're cheating," said Nozzles.

"It's a good thing there are no other monkey's around," said Millard.

"Hey, I didn't cheat," said Sully.

"You're right, Sully. You were the only one who didn't. That's why I've chosen you, to be my nephew for the banquet."

"Did you say, 'nephew?'" said Nozzles.

"Yes," said Millard. "Change of plans. I'm going to be the uncle. Sully will be my nephew."

"Thanks, Millard. That means a lot," said Sully. "Wait a minute. That means no door prize?"

"For you."

"No way!" said Sully. "That's not fair."

"But I chose you to be my nephew, remember?"

"Yeah, well... okay, that still means a lot. I'll do it."

"Great. Put on this monkey mask."

"I can't believe this!" said Nozzles.

"Hey," said Gruffy. "Didn't you do this last year, Millard?"

"And the year before that and the year before that," said Racquet. "I can't believe we fell for it again."

"I'd love to stay and chat," said Millard. "But we've got to get going. The banquet starts in a few minutes."

"How do you know?" said Sully.

"Sniff the air," said Gruffy.

The animals did. "Whoa," they said. "Monkeys."

"How about a piggy-back ride to the banquet, Sully?" said Millard.

"What?" said Sully. "You're the uncle. Shouldn't I be getting the ride?"

"Did I mention you're my favorite nephew?"

"Hop on, Uncle Millard," said Sully.

"Whee!" said Millard. "That door prize is as good as mine!"

"Which way?" said Sully.

"Follow your nose," said Gruffy.

"Welcome to the First Annual Monkey Monthly Uncle/Nephew Monkey Banquet," said the monkey at the door. "Same rules as last year. Which one of you is the nephew?"

"Me," said Sully.

The door monkey's eyes narrowed. "I smell aardvark."

"That's me," said Millard. "I'm the uncle."

"Wow, all of the uncles are aardvarks tonight. But you look like a monkey."

"And I act like one, too," said Millard. "'Scent of Aardvark' is my favorite aftershave. All the monkey uncles are wearing it."

The door monkey scratched his head. "So are you an aardvark or not? You know what? I really don't care. Here are your badgers."

"You mean 'badges?'" said Sully.

"No. Badgers. They'll take you to your table. Careful, the one in front bites. Next."

Sully and Millard followed the badgers.

"And I thought we weren't going to get away with this," said Sully.

"Ouch!" said Millard. "He does bite."

Sully and Millard sat down and looked around. Monkeys and aardvarks were everywhere.

"Ouch!" said Sully.

"Did he bite you?" said Millard.

"No," said Sully. "This monkey mask is hurting my nose."

"Ouch! He bit me again," said Millard. He smiled from ear-to-ear. "I love monkey banquets."

Just then a voice came over the loud speaker. "Attention, uncles." All of the aardvarks looked up except for Sully. "It's time to announce the winner of the door prize."

"Ouch!" said Sully.

"Badger?" said Millard.

"Mask," said Sully.

"Drawing," said the badger. "Shhhhh."

"And the winner is… "

Chapter Five

"And the winner is… hang on, the print's a little small… if my arms were longer I could read it… the uncle of 'Marvin J. Monkey!'"

"Aw," said Millard and Sully, sadly. "Maybe next year." Then Millard remembered. "Wait a minute! I'm Marvin!"

"I thought I was Marvin," said Sully. "I'm the nephew."

"I don't think so, but who cares?" said Millard. "We won! Ouch!"

56.

"Come on up to the stage, Marvin's uncle!" said the announcer monkey. "And bring your nephew. We have a prize for him, too."

Millard and Sully danced their way up the aisle to the stage. They were happy to be away from the biting badger.

"Ouch!" said Sully. My monkey mask still hurts."

"Congratulations, Marvin!" said the announcer monkey.

"Thank you," said Millard and Sully.

"We have two monkeys, folks!" said the announcer. "What are the odds? Which one of you is Marvin?"

"I am," said Millard and Sully. "No, I am," said Millard and Sully. "Don't you remember?" they said to each other. "I do," they said, "but you don't." They looked around. "Oh, boy."

Just then a huge caged dropped down from the ceiling onto them!

"Freeze!" said the badgers. They pulled

off their suits revealing their badges. "Finally caught you in the act." They were all monkey police officers. The aardvarks all pulled off their suits. They were monkey detectives. And the monkeys pulled off their suits. They were all monkey police captains.

Millard and Sully were handcuffed, printed and booked on the spot.

"We've been onto your cheating ways, Marvin, a.k.a. Markie, Maynard, Morrie, Melissa and Millard J. Monkey, for years," said the announcer monkey, a.k.a. The Chief of Police Monkey. "You've always managed to slip through our fingers. But not this time."

"You've got us all wrong, Chief!" said Millard.

"We've got you, all right," said the Chief. "These banquets have all been traps. Well, not the first one. You caught us off guard when you cheated to get that door prize. That's when we knew we had to take you down."

Sully hung his head. "I knew something

58.

was fishy when Millard got invited somewhere."

"It cost the taxpayers a pretty bunch of bananas," said the Chief. "But if there's one thing we monkeys can't stand, it's cheating. And door prize cheaters! The only lower form of life is a free magazine cheater. Yes sir, it's a red-letter day for the force. Take them away, boys. I can't stand to look at them anymore."

That day, Millard and Sully learned about the importance of not cheating. They also learned how to break rocks and stamp license plates.

That day, and for the next three to five years.

A message from Gruffy Bear...

Dum de dum dum dum.

Oh, yeah. Here's more stuff from the jungle
Jungle Jam™ on CD

Each set has nearly five hours of classic episodes on four CDs:
12 radio shows, most with two different stories;
over 20 adventures per set for kids 4 through 74.
(Some material not appropriate for 75-year olds.)

UPC 8-20265-21312-6

Wild Times in God's Creation

Get ready for *Wild Times in God's Creation* with the Jungle Jam gang! Straight from the jungle are berry-eating bears, a selfish squirrel, and a loony monkey and an aardvark battling for the ultimate treasure, a bag of marbles.

More Wild Times in God's Creation

Hey, what do you get when you combine a conconut-clunking monkey, a bear obsessed with finding the perfect picinic spot, and a warthog who wants to be an aardvark?

No, silly, not some wacky Noah's ark party, but *More Wild Times in God's Creation* from the Jungle Jam gang!

UPC 8-20265-21322-5

UPC 8-20265-21332-4

Even Wilder Times in God's Creation

Find out how it all started. Stories with over 50 original songs from these classic Jungle Jam™ recordings:

King of the Jungle
Cheetah Bonita Goes Solo
Three Wise Men and a Baby
All God's Creatures are Special
Fear, Faith and Five Really Big Footprints
and even the RazzleFlabbenz in
Red and Yellow, Black and - Plaid?

To order visit FancyMonkey.com
or call McRuffy Press at 1-888-967-1200

Jungle Jam™ Chapter Books

ISBN 1-59269-002-5

King Liar

A warthog, inner tubes, peanut butter sandwiches, fort-building… what more could you want in a story? How about a silly ape and the Jungle Jam gang? Oh, and maybe a lesson on **truthfulness** from **Proverbs 6:17**.

And **HOW GREEN WAS MY SULLY** is another story in this very same book! Kinda like getting a toy in your favorite cereal. Find out about the **danger of envy** from **James 3:16**.

The Monkey Who Cried "Walrus!"

It is the hottest day of the year, and the Jungle Jam gang has only one thing on their minds: ice pops! The only problem is Millard the monkey has eaten them all! Or has he? Warm up to this cool story about **not judging others** from **Proverbs 17:15**.

And in **TIME TO WATCH THE CLOCK**, Millard volunteers to deliver a clock to Nozzles the elephant - and time may never be the same! At least for that clock. It's a minute-by-minute lesson in **responsibility** for our favorite monkey from **Luke 16:10**.

ISBN 1-59269-000-9

junglejam™

Just because we live in a jungle doesn't mean we have to act like animals